The Princess and the Packet of FROZEN Peas

For my favourite Ps, Pippa and Polly. —T. W.

For my two ugly stepsisters, Sofie and Simone. —S. deG.

Published by
PEACHTREE PUBLISHERS
1700 Chattahoochee Avenue
Atlanta, Georgia 30318-2112
www.peachtree-online.com

Text © 2009 by Tony Wilson
Illustrations © 2009 by Sue deGennaro

First United States edition published in 2012.

Illustrations created in collage, gouache, and pencil.
Typeset in Futura, BlackJack, Linotype Tapeside and Hilde Sharpie.

Printed in October 2011 by Tien Wah Press in Singapore.
10 9 8 7 6 5 4 3 2 1
First Edition

First published in 2009 by Scholastic Australia.

Cataloging-in-Publication data is available from The Library of Congress

ISBN 13: 978-1-56145-635-2 / ISBN 10: 1-56145-635-7

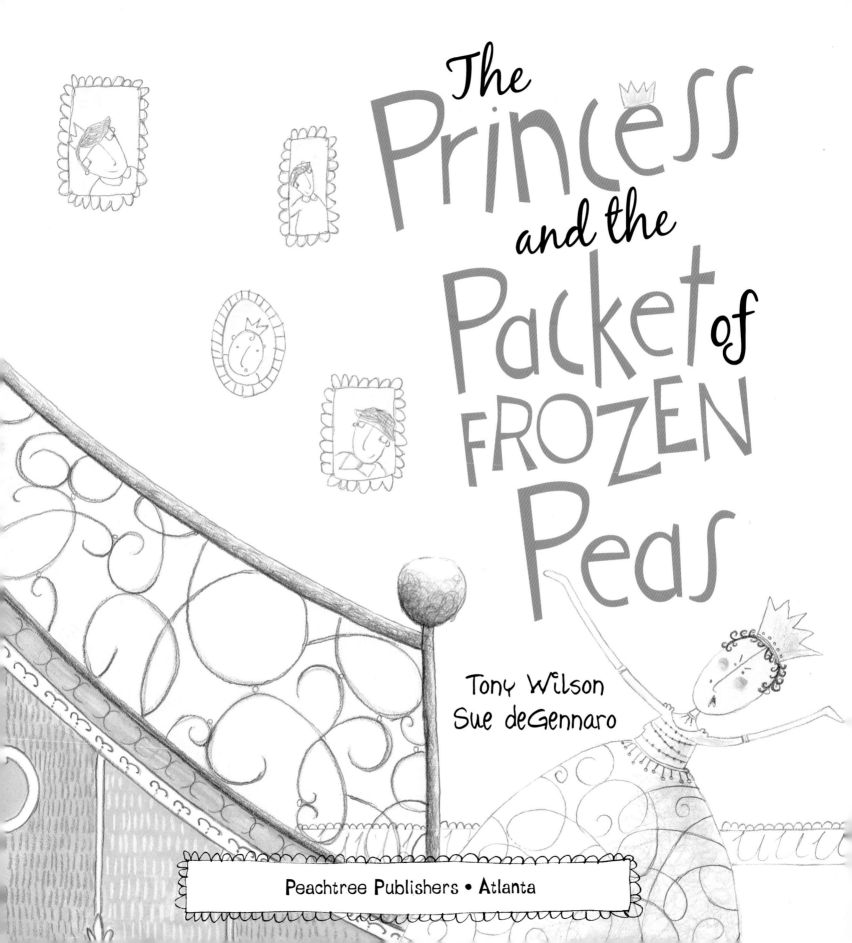

The Princess and the Packet of FROZEN Peas

Tony Wilson
Sue deGennaro

Peachtree Publishers • Atlanta

Once upon a time

there was a **prince** called **Henrik** who wanted very much to fall in *love* and get married.

He was an **outdoorsy** type, and hoped that the *princess* he married would like hockey and camping.

There were many girls who wanted to marry a *prince*. Every time **Henrik** left the palace, groups of screaming girls would yell,

"Oh my goodness, it's him!"

and throw flowers in his general direction.

Henrik decided to ask his brother for advice.

"The most important thing is to make sure she is a *real princess*," Prince Hans said.

"A real princess is very *beautiful* and very *sensitive*. When I met my wife, *Princess Eva*, I made a stack of twenty mattresses and twenty eiderdown quilts. Then I put a single pea under the bottom mattress. If a girl complains about feeling the pea through mattresses and eiderdown quilts, she must be a *real princess*."

"Did *Princess Eva* complain?" **Prince Henrik** asked.
"You bet—she complained a lot," said *Prince Hans*.

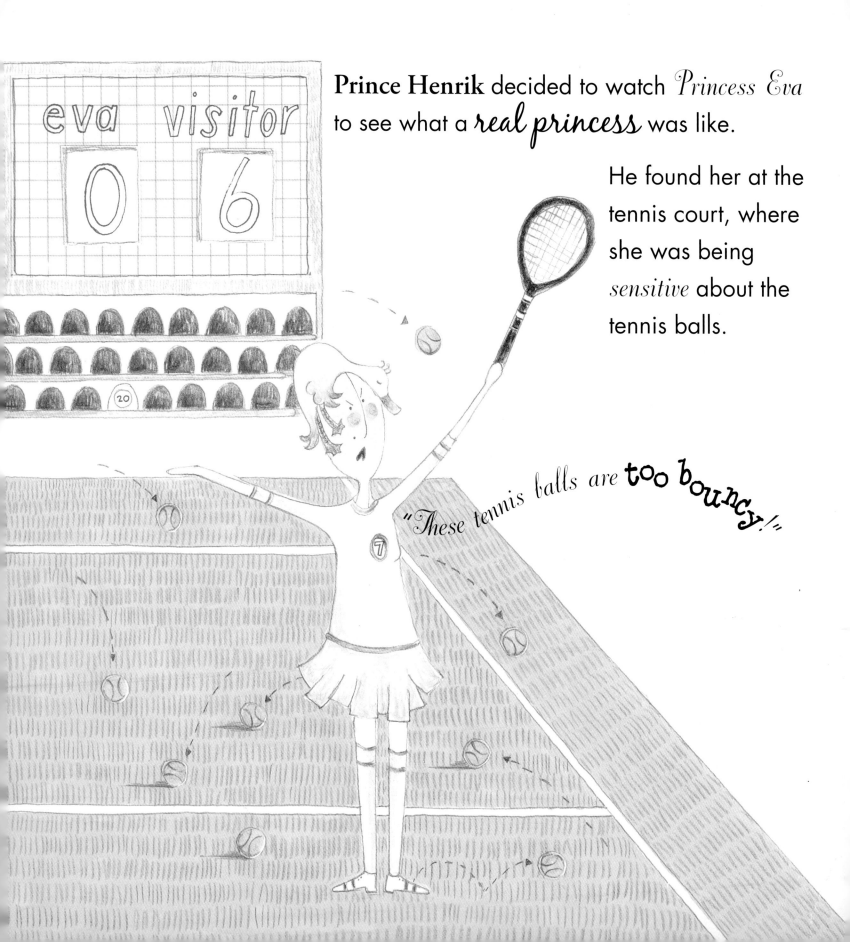

eva visitor

0 6

Prince Henrik decided to watch *Princess Eva* to see what a **real princess** was like.

He found her at the tennis court, where she was being *sensitive* about the tennis balls.

"These tennis balls are **too bouncy!**"

He followed her to the driveway and saw her being *sensitive* about her new sports car.

"This isn't the car I wanted! I wanted one with drink holders. And yellow!"

Prince Henrik wondered whether perhaps
Princess Eva was a little too *sensitive.*

Prince Henrik decided he didn't want to marry a *real princess* like *Princess Eva*. He wanted to marry the exact opposite.

She didn't have to be *beautiful* or *sensitive*. She just had to like hockey and camping and have a nice smile.

And so **Prince Henrik** came up with a plan.

Whenever a *girl* came to stay,
    he offered to make up the guest room.

Instead of twenty mattresses,
    Henrik found one thin camping mattress.

Instead of twenty eiderdown quilts,
    Henrik found one old sleeping bag.

And instead of a single pea,
    the **prince** decided to use a whole
    packet of FROZEN PEAS.

Many young girls visited, but none passed the test.

"You won't believe this.
I found PEAS in my bed."

"I couldn't sleep at all!
There was a massive
lump under the mattress."

"What's the deal with the
packet of FROZEN PEAS?"

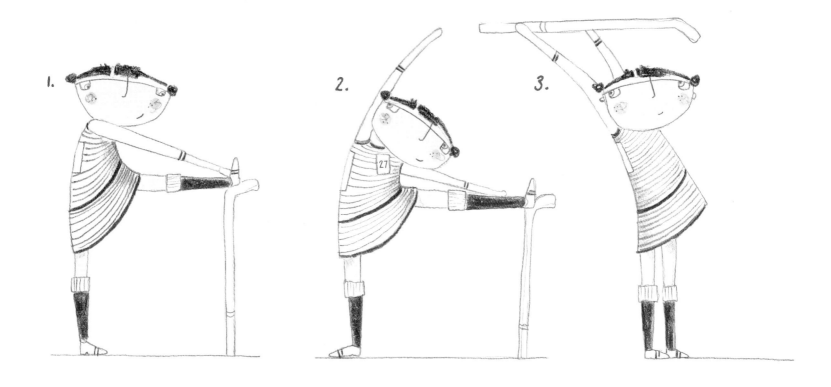

Then one morning **Henrik**'s old friend **Pippa** came to stay.

They had a great day riding horses, playing hockey, and spying on *Princess Eva* as she complained about everything in the *palace*.

"If she's a *real princess*," Henrik joked, "I want to marry the opposite."

Henrik and **Pippa** laughed. For the first time **Prince Henrik** noticed what a lovely laugh his friend had.

That night
 he decided to test her with
  the packet of FROZEN PEAS.

The following
morning
Henrik sat in
the corridor
outside the
guest room.

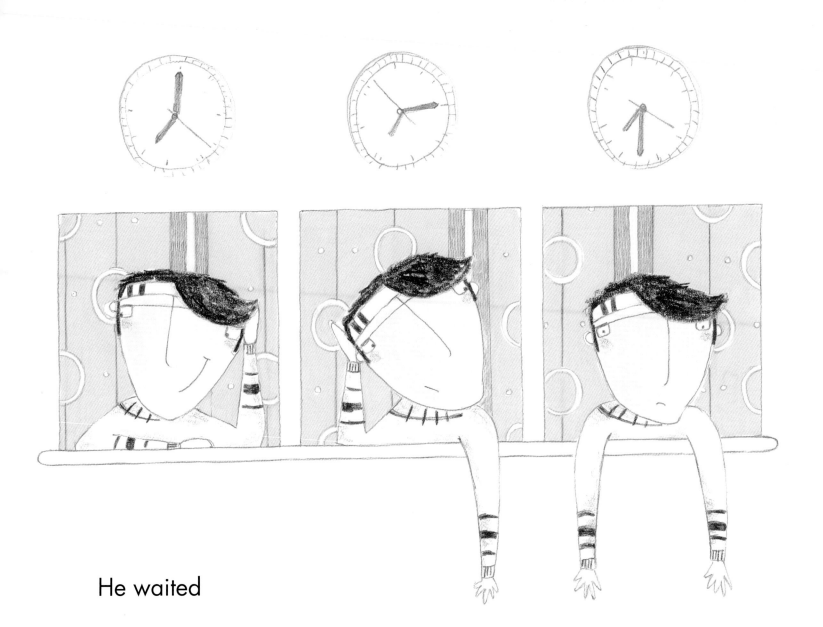

He waited

and waited

and waited.

Finally, **Pippa** emerged, yawning.

"How did you sleep?"
asked **Henrik**.

"Fantastically well, thank you."
Pippa handed him a packet of mushy peas.

"I found this under the mattress last night," she said.

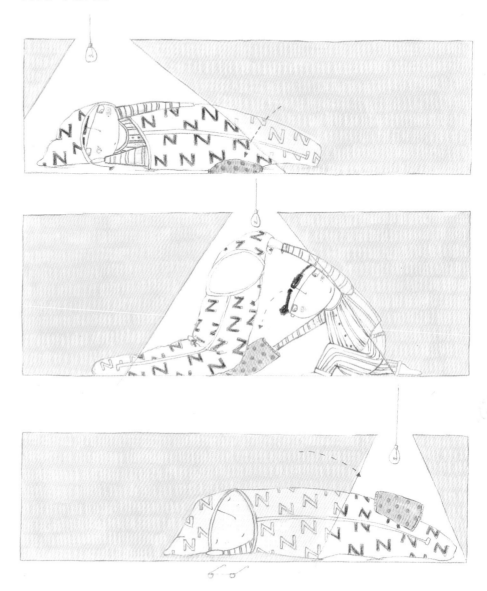

"It was the perfect ice pack. I had a bit of a sore shin from playing hockey."

The **prince** beamed. **Pippa** beamed back.

She had a lovely gap between her two front teeth.

"Will you marry me?" asked **Prince Henrik**.

"But I'm not a real princess," Pippa answered.

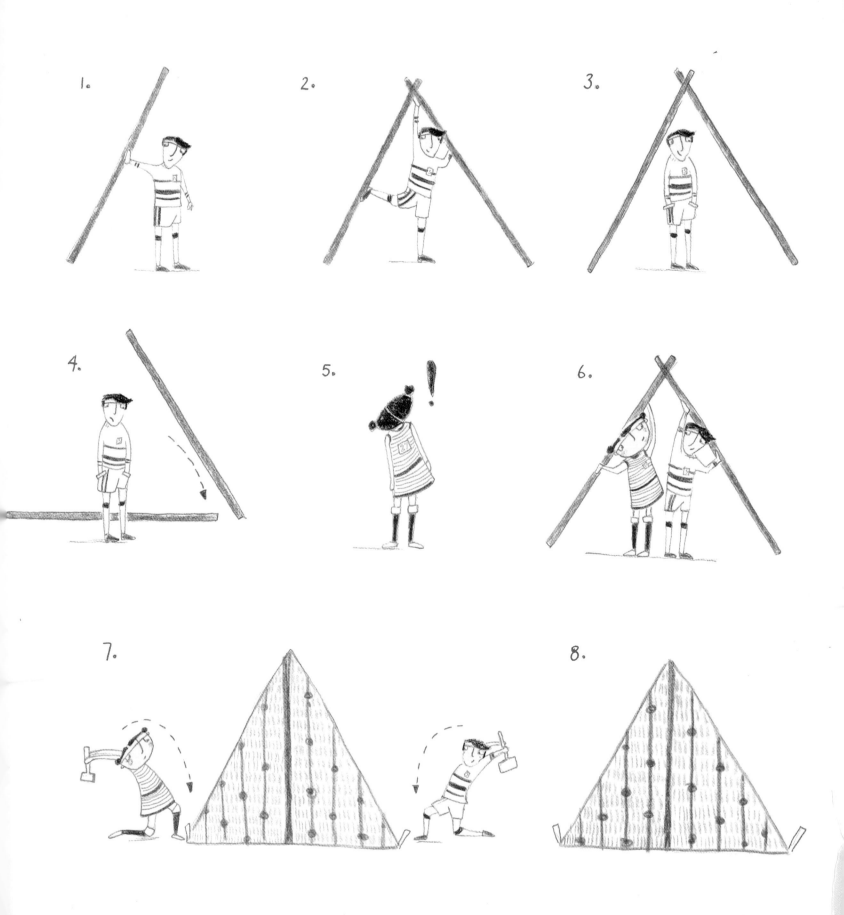

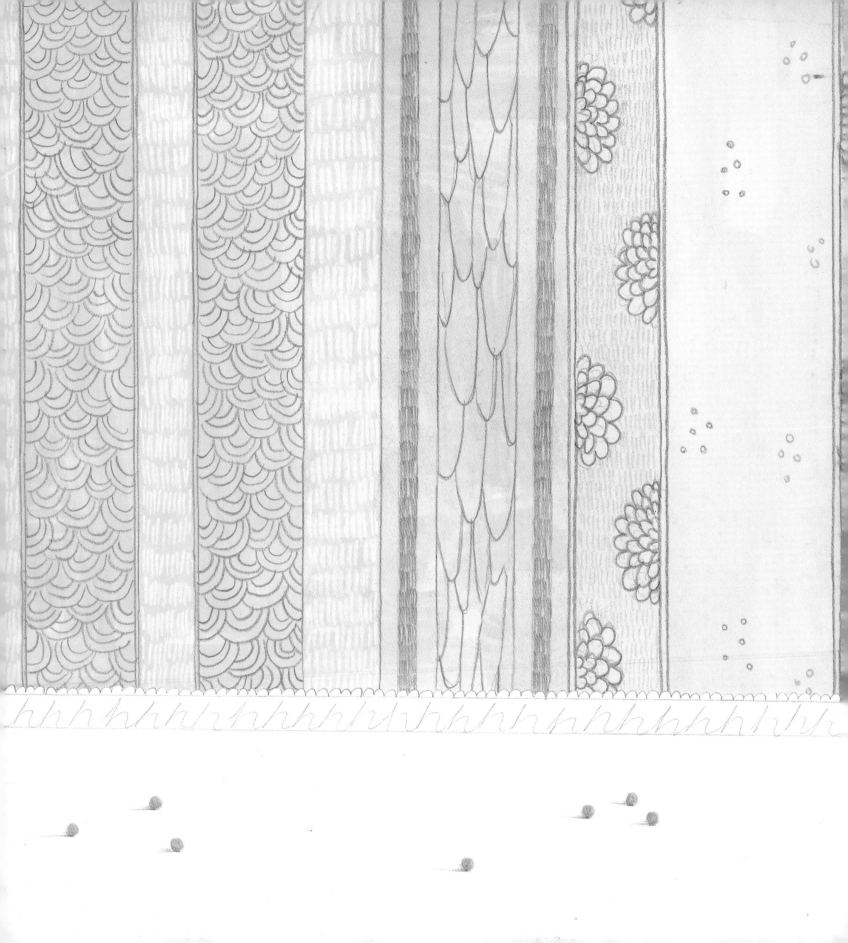